W9-BUM-900

TINY
GOES TO THE LIBRARY

A Viking Easy-to-Read

by
Cari Meister

illustrated by
Rich Davis

VIKING

For Judy, the best editor
in the whole wide world.
—C.M.

To Angie, my wife and best friend:
I'm so glad God brought us together
to make a home. I love you!
—R.D.

VIKING
Published by the Penguin Group
Penguin Putnam Inc., 345 Hudson Street, New York, New York 10014, U.S.A.
Penguin Books Ltd, 27 Wrights Lane, London W8 5TZ, England

Penguin Books Ltd, Registered Offices: Harmondsworth, Middlesex, England

First published in 2000 by Viking and Puffin Books,
divisions of Penguin Putnam Books for Young Readers

3 5 7 9 10 8 6 4

Text copyright © Cari Meister, 2000
Illustrations copyright © Rich Davis, 2000
All rights reserved

Library of Congress Cataloging-in-Publication Data
Meister, Cari.
Tiny goes to the library / by Cari Meister : illustrated by Rich Davis.
p. cm. — (A Viking easy-to-read)
Summary: Tiny the dog is a big help at the library when his owner takes out too many
books to carry home.
ISBN 0-670-88556-8 (hc) — ISBN 0-14-130488-X (pbk)
[I. Libraries—Fiction 2. Books and reading—Fiction. 3. Dogs—Fiction.] I. Davis, Rich,
date– ill. II. Title. III. Series.
PZ7.M515916 Tg 2000 [E]—dc21 98-051134

Printed in Hong Kong
Set in Bookman

Viking® and Easy-to-Read® are registered trademarks of Penguin Putnam Inc.

Without limiting the rights under copyright reserved above, no part of this publication
may be reproduced, stored in or introduced into a retrieval system, or transmitted, in
any form or by any means (electronic, mechanical, photocopying, recording or otherwise),
without the prior written permission of both the copyright owner and the above
of this book.

Reading level 1.3

TINY
GOES TO THE LIBRARY

This is Tiny.

He is my best friend.

He goes where I go.

If I go to the park, Tiny comes, too.

If I go to the lake, Tiny comes, too.

Today we are going to the library.

I get my library card.

I get my wagon.

Time to go!

Sorry, Tiny.

No dogs in the library.

You wait here.

I go inside.

Tiny stays outside.

I get dog books.

I get frog books.

I get bird books for Tiny.

I fill the wagon.

Tiny helps.

Oh no! Too many books!

I cannot pull the wagon.

Tiny can!

Stop, Tiny, stop!

Wait for me!

Go, Tiny, go!

Good dog, Tiny.

DISCARDED